John F. Burrowes

The thorough-Bass Primer

containing explanations and examples of the rudiments of harmony,

comprising the fifty preliminary excercises from

John F. Burrowes

The thorough-Bass Primer
containing explanations and examples of the rudiments of harmony, comprising the fifty preliminary excercises from

ISBN/EAN: 9783337390433

Printed in Europe, USA, Canada, Australia, Japan

Cover: Foto ©Andreas Hilbeck / pixelio.de

More available books at **www.hansebooks.com**

THE

THOROUGH-BASS PRIMER;

CONTAINING

EXPLANATIONS AND EXAMPLES

OF THE

RUDIMENTS OF HARMONY,

COMPRISING THE

FIFTY PRELIMINARY EXERCISES FROM "THE COMPANION"
TO THE THOROUGH BASS PRIMER, IN ADDITION
TO THE ORIGINAL FIFTY EXERCISES, APPER-
TAINING TO THE PRIMER.

BY

J. F. BURROWES.

FIFTIETH EDITION.
ENLARGED, REVISED AND CORRECTED.

BOSTON:
OLIVER DITSON & COMPANY.
NEW YORK: C. H. DITSON & CO.—CHICAGO: LYON & HEALY.

Entered according to Act of Congress, in the year 1874, by O. Ditson & Co., in the
Office of the Librarian of Congress, at Washington.

PREFACE.

THE present modified and improved edition of BUR-
ROWES's THOROUGH-BASS PRIMER comprises, in addition
to the Exercises appertaining to the original edition, those
also contained in the companion to the THOROUGH-BASE
PRIMER by the same author, interspersed throughout the
work in the order in which they are required to illustrate
the rules introduced in the course of instruction. In its
present form it is confidently believed the THOROUGH-BASS
PRIMER will prove more acceptable to teachers and learners
than previous editions, inasmuch as it will save both time
and trouble in turning from book to book.

It is, as the Title implies, an Elementary Work, not
treating of Counterpoint, Rhythm, &c., and is only intended
to enable the student to understand and accompany figured
Bases, which is as far as many wish to proceed.

The Author has endeavored to render the explanations
as simple as possible; and in order to save the time of the
Teacher, as well as to impress them on the mind of the Student, has accompanied the explanation of each chord with
progressive exercises; which plan, if not new, he hopes
will be found useful.

The Exercises are not offered as specimens of composition, being merely calculated to introduce the chords as they
are explained, while for the sake of practice, the modulations are frequently made very abrupt. Besides those
which are inserted, the pupil will find it a very excellent
plan at different periods of his study to accompany the scale
in various keys, sometimes taking it for a melody and sometimes for a base. An exercise may also be copied without
the figures, and the chords changed; or discords by suspension inserted to the chords already marked. This, however, must be done at the discretion of the Teacher, whose
judgment necessarily directs a mode of instruction suited to
the capacity of his Pupil, and whose experience may dictate
to one individual a course which may be inexpedient for
another.

CONTENTS.

A. B. KIDDER & SON'S MUSIC TYPOGRAPHY.

THOROUGH - BASS PRIMER.

INTRODUCTION.

Pupils who intend to study this book should first be well acquainted with a rudimental knowledge of music, such as is contained in Burrowes' Pianoforte Primer and Catechisms in general; particularly with the Major and Minor Third, Perfect Fifth, and Leading-note of every Key; also with the formation and connection of Major and Minor scales and their respective signatures. See following illustrations.

THE DIATONIC SCALE

consists of a series of Tones and Half-tones (Steps and Half-steps) in the following order :

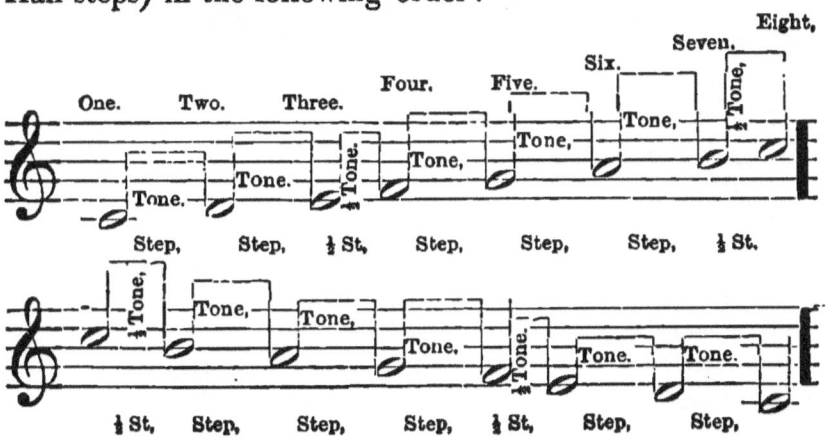

In Thorough-Bass they are generally named Tonic, Super-tonic, Mediant, Sub-dominant, Dominant, Sub-mediant, Leading-note and Tonic. *Eight* being an acute reproduction of *one*, it has the same name.

DIATONIC SCALE.

KEY OF C MAJOR.

SCALE OF RELATIVE A MINOR.

CHROMATIC SCALE.

Q. How many *sounds* are there in the Diatonic Scale?

Eight, called respectively one, two, three, four, five, six, seven, eight.

Q. How many *tones* or *steps?*

Five, as follows: Between one and two, two and three, four and five, five and six, six and seven.

Q. How many *semitones* or *half-steps?*

Two, between three and four, seven and eight.

Q. In what respect does a Minor Scale differ from its relative Major Scale?

It is two degrees lower, and requires the seventh to be raised a semitone or half-step; consequently in the succession of tones and semitones (steps and half-steps) it differs materially from the Major.

Q. Why is a Minor Scale said to be relative to a Major Scale?
Because it has the same signature.

Give examples of scales in other Keys, with their proper signatures.

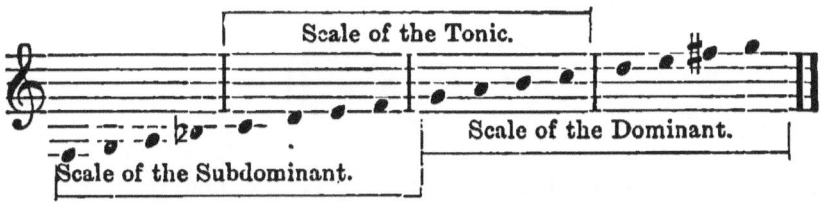

Give an example in the Key of G, D, A, or any other key with flats
or sharps at the signature.

Name any one in the ORDER of keys with sharps or flats at the signature, not beyond C♯, which has seven sharps or C♭, which has
seven flats. The pupil no doubt is aware — (See Pianoforte Primer,
Exercises 10 and 11) — that beyond these keys, double sharps or flats
would be requisite; and though frequently used in the course of modulation, they are never placed at the signature, for this reason — all
those keys which require them are called by different names; thus the
key of A♯, which would require ten sharps, (three double and four
single,) is called B♭, and has two flats; the key of B♯ would require
twelve sharps — is called the key of C, which has neither flats nor '
sharps; and the same is to be observed of all those keys beyond C♯
or C♭.

INTERVALS.

THERE are two modes of reckoning Intervals. The one
is to count the number of *sounds;* the other, to count the
number of *semitones.* The following explanation, it is
hoped, will enable the student to understand both methods.

An INTERVAL is the distance or difference *between* two
SOUNDS.

The smallest Interval upon the Pianoforte, (to which
instrument all the explanations in this book relate) is a
SEMITONE or HALF-STEP.

Each key of the piano-forte is a semitone from that
which is next to it, whether it be a white key or a black
one.

A semitone is called *chromatic* when it *retains* its name
and degree upon the Staff, as C, C♯, &c.

A semitone is called *diatonic* when it changes its **name** and degree upon the staff, as C, D♭, &c.

All intervals are called according to the number of letters or degrees of the staff, thus: —

is not called a second (although C♯ is the second sound of the chromatic scale) because both sounds are called C, and are upon the same degree of the staff; but

is called a second, because D is the second letter of the Diatonic Scale of C, and is upon the next degree of the staff from C.

Those intervals which have no other designation than a *number*, as second, third, fifth, &c., applied to them, are to be sharp, flat, or natural, according to the scale which is under consideration; for example, in the *key of C* the second of the scale is D, the third of the scale is E, &c.; but in the *key of E* the second of the scale is F♯, the third of the scale is G♯, &c. This rule also holds good when intervals are reckoned in other parts of the scale, as well as from the tonic: thus in the *key of C* the third from D is F; but in the *key of G* the third of D is F♯.

Those intervals which have accidentals prefixed to them must be raised or lowered from their original places in the scale, according as they are marked.

To prove whether any interval be major or minor, it is necessary to reckon all the *intermediate sounds*, (viz., every sound of the chromatic scale.) If the number of sounds be counted, they will be one greater than the number of *Semitones*: thus in reckoning from A to C♯, the number of sounds (of the chromatic scale) is five, although C♯ is only four semitones from A.

They must be reckoned thus : *from* A to A♯ is one semi-tone, to B two, to C three, to C♯ four.

Thirds, fifths and leading-notes, being the only intervals usually explained in the rudiments, the author now recommends the pupil to study attentively the following

TABLE OF INTERVALS.

Tonic.

Unison.

which signifies the SAME SOUND produced by two or more instruments or voices,—

A unison is not an interval, for it must be remembered that an interval is the *difference* between *two* sounds.

The 2d Sound of the Chromatic Scale is

An augmented Prime or Chromatic semitone.

One Semitone from the Tonic, Key note, or Root.

The 2d Sound is also called

Minor Second.*

One Semitone from Tonic.

*It is to be observed that, although the same Keys on the Piano-forte and other keyed Instruments are used for C♯ and D♭, &c., &c., it is not the case with instruments in general.

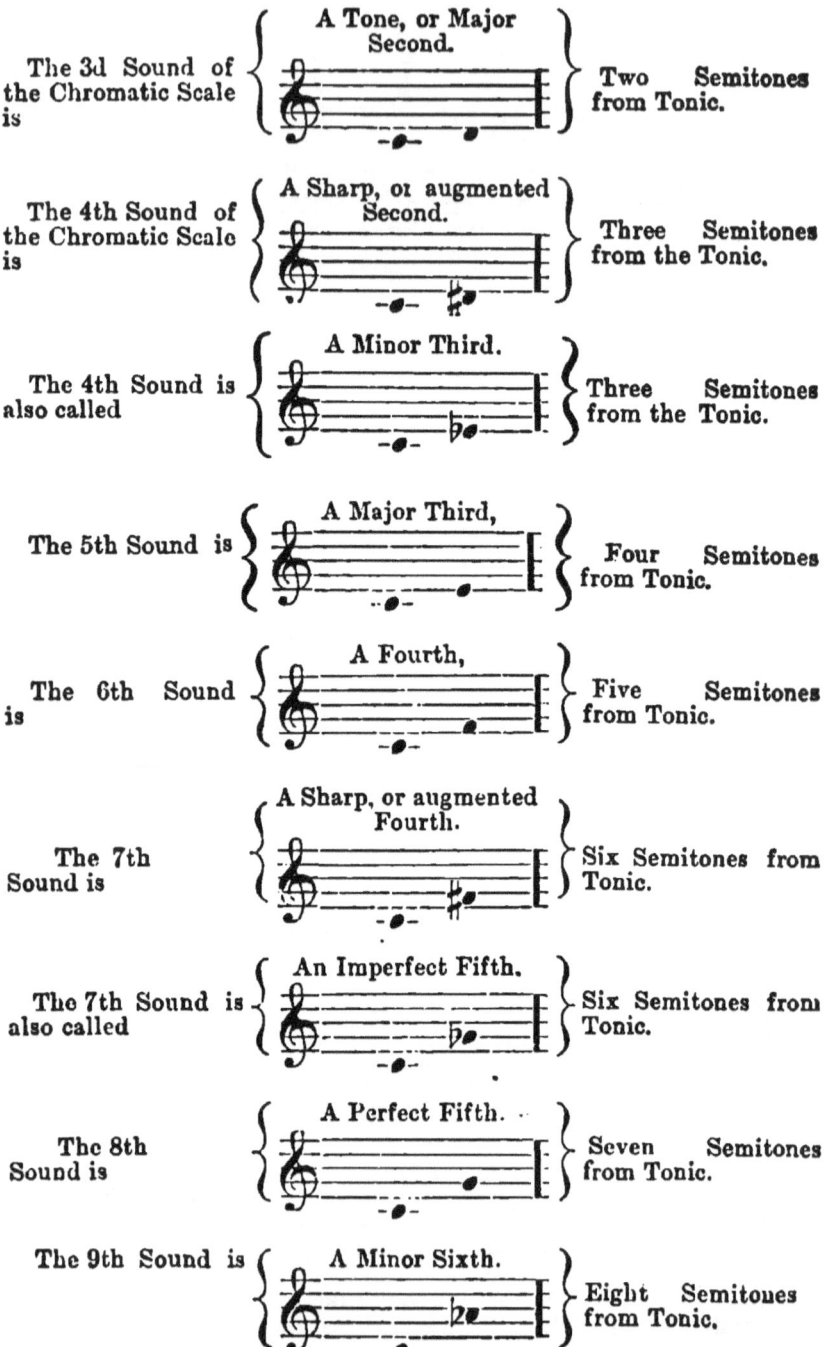

The 3d Sound of the Chromatic Scale is — A Tone, or Major Second. — Two Semitones from Tonic.

The 4th Sound of the Chromatic Scale is — A Sharp, or augmented Second. — Three Semitones from the Tonic.

The 4th Sound is also called — A Minor Third. — Three Semitones from the Tonic.

The 5th Sound is — A Major Third, — Four Semitones from Tonic.

The 6th Sound is — A Fourth, — Five Semitones from Tonic.

The 7th Sound is — A Sharp, or augmented Fourth. — Six Semitones from Tonic.

The 7th Sound is also called — An Imperfect Fifth. — Six Semitones from Tonic.

The 8th Sound is — A Perfect Fifth. — Seven Semitones from Tonic.

The 9th Sound is — A Minor Sixth. — Eight Semitones from Tonic.

The 10th Sound is	A Major Sixth,	Nine Semitones from Tonic.
The 11th Sound is	A sharp, or augmented, Sixth.	Ten Semitones from Tonic.
The 11th Sound is also called	A Minor Seventh.	Ten Semitones from Tonic.
The 12th Sound is	A Major Seventh, or Leading-note,	Eleven Semitones from Tonic.
The 13th Sound is	An Octave,	Twelve Semitones from Tonic.
The 14th Sound is	A Flat, or Minor Ninth	Thirteen Semitones from Tonic.
The 15th Sound is	A Major Ninth.	Fourteen Semitones from Tonic.

Write or repeat a Table of Intervals similar to the preceding, reckoning from E, E♭, B, or any other note, instead of C.

Intervals are not usually reckoned beyond a ninth, as the terms *tenth, eleventh, twelfth, &c.*, which were formerly applied to the *octave* above the *third, fourth, fifth, &c.*, being a repetition of former sounds, they are distinguished by the name of Compound Intervals: for example, any E is called the third, any F the fourth, or any G the fifth of C, however distant they may be from each other and the tonic, from which they are counted. Intervals are counted upwards (from the lowest note to the highest) when not otherwise indicated.

INVERSION OF INTERVALS.

THE Inversion of an Interval signifies either putting the highest note an Octave lower, or the lowest note an Octave higher, while the other remains in its original place.

The easiest method of showing what any interval will become when inverted, is to add as many to the number by which it is called as will make up *nine*, — the difference will give the name of the interval when inverted : thus a unison (which is represented by the number one) will, being inverted, become an eighth ; a second will become a seventh ; a third will become a sixth, &c., &c. For example : —

THOROUGH-BASS.

A MELODY is a succession of single musical sounds which can be produced by a single voice or instrument. Two or more different Sounds, heard simultaneously, are called HARMONY. These Sounds are derived from what is termed the ROOT, the RADICAL BASS, or FUNDAMENTAL BASS. As it would be monotonous to use none but radical bases, other bases, *derived from them*, are frequently used. Thorough-Bass is the application of harmony to a figured bass (that is, a bass with figures annexed denoting the harmony designed to accompany it.) The rules which govern the application of the notes, intervals, or harmony indicated by such figures, in their relations to the bass and to each other, constitute what is termed Thorough-Bass.

CHAPTER I.

THE COMMON CHORD.

Q. Of how many sounds does a Common Chord or Triad consist?

Three; *viz.,* a Bass note or Tonic with its third and fifth.

Name the notes which form the common chord of **A**, of **B, C, D, E, F, G.**

Q. Is not the octave to the bass generally added?

Yes.

Q. In how many positions can the common chord be taken?

Three; for example : —

Q. What is the difference between a Major Common Chord and a Minor Common Chord?

The difference is in the *Third;* for example : — if the third be major, it is a major chord; if the third be minor, it is a minor chord; the fifth in both cases must be perfect.

Write out the following exercises, adding the deficient notes belonging to each chord, observing that nothing is to be written higher than the given note in each chord. When properly corrected, play the exercise as written. Afterwards play it from the original copy, supplying the deficient notes without referring to the manuscript or key. The same should be done with all the succeeding exercises.

2

Write and play major chords in three positions to Exercise and Study I. Commence with either the third, fifth, or octave uppermost, and put the two other notes in the nearest positions of the chord, either ascending or descending. Mark each Interval* with a figure as in the foregoing example.

Write and play minor chords in the same manner to Exercise and Study I.

Preliminary Exercise I.   Major Chords in three positions.

Study I.

Q. As the octave to the bass is generally added, may either of the other sounds be doubled?

Yes; for instance, in the chord of C as many Cs, Es and Gs may be written as the student chooses, bearing in mind that it is better to double the octave than either of the others, and the fifth rather than the third.

Q. As the common chord may be taken in three positions, is the student at liberty to take which he pleases?

If a melody be given (as in Exercise II.,) nothing should be written above it; but if there be no melody given, he may take the chords in whatever position he thinks will produce the best effect.

Q. What are the progressions to be avoided in writing or playing chords?

Those which produce consecutive Fifths or Octaves; that is to say, one part must not move in fifths or octaves with another; the progression, therefore, of each note, must be considered.† For example:—

---

*After writing a few chords, it will be sufficient to mark the upper note only.

†A musical composition is said to be in so many parts, moving in proper progression. When speaking of parts, voice-parts are to be understood, as the rules for their progression apply more strictly than in any other form of writing.

The G in the first bar, which is a fifth from C, must not move to A, which is the fifth of D. The G in the second bar, being the fifth of C, must not move to E, which is the fifth of A. The upper and lower E, in the third bar, must not both move to F, as that makes consecutive octaves. The following example is in four parts —

and must be analyzed in this way : —The first part or the melody is B, C ; the second part G, A, which are consecutive octaves with the bass ; and the third part, D, E, are consecutive fifths with the bass. These faults may be avoided by altering either the first or second chord, thus :

In the following example the faults are avoided and the melody retained.

The upper part is still B, C, the second part G, E, and the third part D, C, neither of which move in fifths or octaves with the bass, or with either of the other parts.

Write and play Common Chords to Exercise II. and Study II.

Q. How is the performer to decide whether a major or a minor chord is to be played?

From the signature, for no accidentals must be used unless they are indicated. In all major keys the tonic, sub-dominant,* and dominant have major chords; the second, third, and sixth of the scale have minor chords; but the seventh or leading-note cannot have a common chord, as it bears an imperfect fifth.

---

* It has already been shown, that the fifth below by inversion becomes the fourth above; the pupil, however, is advised for the future to consider the sub-dominant as the fourth, and the dominant the fifth of the tonic.

† This example is inserted to show that a common chord may be

2*

Q. When there is no melody given, what are the best general rules to observe in writing or playing chords to the Exercises ?

Generally to begin and end each exercise with the octave of the bass at the top; also, to move the chords as little as possible; that is, when there are any sounds in one chord which belong to the next, they should be retained in the next chord; thus : —

&c.

These rules, however, are by no means invariable.

Q. Upon what progression of the bass is it most necessary to guard against making consecutive fifths and octaves ?

When the bass moves only one degree, they are more likely to be made than by any other progression. The surest mode of avoiding them is to make the chords move in a contrary direction to the bass, unless the melody or some other reason prevent it. See pages 16 and 17.

Q. Are there any other restrictions to be observed in the progression of the notes of the common chord, besides the avoidance of consecutive fifths and octaves ?

All the notes of the common chord may move at the discretion of the player, except the *major* third, which, *if possible*, should ascend one degree. In the foregoing example, the major third of C, (E, in the first chord,) cannot ascend, because there is no F in the following chord. The major third of G,(B, in the fifth chord,)however, should and does ascend one degree, there being a C in the following chord.

---

taken to every note of the scale, except the seventh ; but the chords must not be played in succession, as above written, on account of the consecutive fifths and octaves, (which the pupil should point out by way of exercise.) Add to this, the chords follow each other inharmoniously, as there is no sound in one chord which belongs to the next. See Exercise II., in which this is avoided except in one instance.

Write and play chords to Exercise III. and Study III., pointing out which are major and which are minor chords.

Exercise III.

Study III.

Q. It has been remarked, on page 15, that any sound belonging to a common chord may be doubled without altering the nature of the chord; is the student then at liberty to accompany some bass notes with two, and others with three or more notes?

This will depend greatly on the effect intended to be produced, as some passages require a fuller accompaniment than others; but, generally speaking, all the chords of a passage should consist of the same number of notes or parts, and the progression of each part ought to .be as clearly defined as if the piece were written in score. (See pages 92, 93.)

Q. If the same number of parts are employed throughout a passage or composition, how does it happen that some chords appear to consist of a note less than others; thus : —

The second chord really consists of the same number of parts as the first, because the upper C is doubled, in order that the major third of G (*i. e.*, B) may ascend; if sung by four voices, *two* persons would sing the upper C, in which case the progression would be,

The highest part,   D—C
The second part,   B—C
The third part,   G—E
The Bass,   G—C

Some teachers make their pupils write the four parts; thus : —

which is a very good plan, until the student is thoroughly acquainted with the progression of each note, when it may be discontinued.

Write and play Exercise IV. and Study IV.

Exercise IV.

Chords of the Tonic and Attendant Harmonies in major keys.

Chords of the Tonic and attendant Harmonies in minor keys.

Scales.

Study IV.

CHAPTER II.

THE TONIC AND ATTENDANT HARMONIES.

Q. What is meant by the Harmony of the Tonic?

It signifies the common chord of the key-note.

Q. What are the attendant harmonies?

They are the common chords of the sub-dominant and dominant; thus the attendant harmonies of the key of C are F and G.

Ex. First make the signature, then write and play the chord of the tonic and the attendant harmonies to the following keys, as in the foregoing example.

C, G, D, A, E, B, F♯, C♯,
C F, B♭, E♭, A♭, D♭, G♭, C♭,

Q. As it appears that the chords of the tonic, sub-dominant, and dominant are all major chords in a major key, are they all minor chords in a minor key?

No; the third in the chord of the dominant is made

major by an accidental, by which it is made the leading-
note of the scale; but the chords of the tonic and sub-dominant are both minor.

Tonic.   Sub-dom.   Dom.

Write the signatures to the following minor keys, then write and
play the chords of the tonic and attendant harmonics.

A, E, B, F♯, C♯, G♯, D♯, A♯,
A, D, G, C,   F,   B♭, E♭, A♭.

[After having written and played the chords as above directed, it is
desirable that the pupil should practice playing the chords of the
tonic and attendant harmonics in any major or minor key, without
writing them. In doing this it will not be necessary to think of the
signature, but merely remember that the chords are to be major in a
major key, and minor in a minor key, excepting the dominant, which
is, in all cases, to be a major chord.]

The chords of the tonic, sub-dominant, and dominant include all
the notes of the scale; consequently the root of each note will be
found in one or other of these three chords.

In the key of C, for example, the C is the root of C, E, and G;
the sub-dominant F, is the root of F, A, and C; and the dominant G,
is the root of G, B, and D.

If the scale be taken for a melody, and accompanied by these three
chords, it is best to consider the fifth to be derived from the tonic, as
it prevents the harshness which arises from taking the chord of G
between two chords of F.

Ex. Make the signature of the key of C, F, A♭, G, B, and D.
Write the scale for a melody; put the root or fundamental bass to
each note, and afterwards fill up the harmony by the common chords.

[Should the pupil find any difficulty in putting the roots to the
scale, the following method will perhaps render it easy :—Write down
the three roots, viz., the tonic, sub-dominant, and dominant, and put
the letters which form their common chords above them. Write, for
instance, the scale of C :—

```
          g,          c,          d,
          e,          a,          b,
The Roots are——C——F——G,
```

The small letters above the capitals are their common chords. The lowest note of the column must be set down as the root. C being the tonic, must, of course, be set down as the root of the first and eighth, although there is a C in the chord of the sub-dominant; and it (C) must also be considered as the root of the fifth of the scale (G), for the reason given above.]

In putting chords to the sixth and seventh of the scale, care must be taken to avoid making consecutive fifths and octaves with the bass (as in the above Ex.) This may be done by making the notes which accompany the leading-note move thus :—

Q. As the figures $\frac{5}{3}$ express the common chord, why are they not placed over the bass notes in the preceding exercises ?

If every bass note were fully figured, it would be difficult to read quickly enough to play the chords from them ; therefore the figures which express the common chord are only used to contradict others which may have preceded them, or when any interval of the chord requires an accidental.

Q. Is it then to be understood that those bass notes which have no figures are to be accompanied with their respective common chords?

Certainly; and it must also be observed that when only

one of these figures is used, the others are implied, thus—

8 8 5
5 3, 3, 8, 5, 3, or a bass note without figures sig-
3,

nifies that the common chord is intended.

Q. What is meant by a ♯, ♭, or ♮ placed over or under a bass note?

It signifies that the *third* of that bass note is to be sharp, flat, or natural, as marked.

Write and play Exercise V. and Study V, and observe that whenever a note which is raised or lowered by an accidental is of the same name as a note in the preceding chord, it must be found in the *same part* of both chords; for instance:—

Exercise V.

Study V.

3

And not

Supposing the above example to be sung by three voices, the same person who sings G in the first chord must sing G♯ in the next.

Q. Does an Accidental *under* another figure thus—$\frac{5}{\#}\,\frac{8}{\natural}$ still relate to the third?

Yes; for example $\frac{5}{\#}$ signifies a fifth and *sharp third*; $\frac{7}{b}$ signifies a seventh and *flat third*, &c.

Q. What is meant by an accidental placed before any figure?

It signifies that the interval is to be sharp, flat, or natural. Thus ♭7 means a *flat seventh*; ♮6 means a *Natural Sixth*, &c.

Q. What is meant by a dash, ascending to the right, drawn through a figure?

It is another method of indicating that the interval so marked is to be sharp. Thus ⚡ means a *sharp fourth*; ⚡ means a *sharp seventh*, &c.

Q. What is meant by a dash after a figure, thus, $\begin{array}{c}5\text{—}\\3\text{—}\end{array}$

It is a mark of continuation, and signifies that the harmony indicated by the preceding figures is still retained; it is also occasionally used when the bass note is changed, to denote that the same chord is to be played as before, notwithstanding the change of the bass; as example:—

Write and play Exercise VI. and Study VI.

Exercise VI.

Exercise I.   Major Chords and their derivatives.

Minor Chords and their derivatives.

Study VI.

Q. In full chords what interval is it most desirable to double?

The octave or fifth should be doubled in preference to the third, because the proper progression of the major third is to ascend one degree; consequently, if doubled, consecutive octaves would occur, or one of the thirds must descend, which produces an unpleasant effect.

Q. What interval in a common chord is it least desirable to omit?

The Third, because the omission of that interval renders it uncertain whether a major or a minor chord is intended. If a bass note be accompanied with only two notes, the third and fifth are most desirable, or third and octave in preference to fifth and octave.

CHAPTER III.

THE DERIVATIVES OR INVERSIONS OF THE COMMON CHORD.

Q. How many chords are derived from the common chord?

Two; the chord of the sixth and the chord of the sixth and fourth.

Q. How is the chord of the sixth produced?

By taking the third instead of the root itself in the bass, thus:—

The root or fundamental bass of each of these chords is C.

Q. How is the chord of the $\frac{6}{4}$ produced?

By taking the fifth instead of the root for a bass, thus—

The root of each of these three chords is C.

Q. Is the performer at liberty to take these and all other chords in what position he pleases, as in the common chord?

Yes; provided the rules (which will be progressively explained) are not broken.

Ex. Write and play a major chord and its two inversions to each note of Exercise I.; remarking, that when the third is taken for a bass, the chord 6 is produced; and when the fifth is taken for a bass, the chord $\frac{6}{4}$ is produced.

3*

Ex. Write and play a minor chord and its two inversions to each note of Exercise I. ; remarking, &c., as before.

Q. When a bass note is marked with a 6, where is the fundamental bass to be found ?

A bass note marked with a 6 is to be considered as the third of its root, consequently the root is a third below.

Q. When a bass note is marked with the figures $\frac{6}{4}$ where is the root to be found ?

A bass note marked $\frac{6}{4}$ is to be considered as the fifth of its root, consequently the fundamental bass is a fifth below.

The following Studies are to be copied on the middle one of three staves ; the upper staff for the chords, the next for the derived bass, (that is the bass which is to be played,) and the lowest for the fundamental bass, which is to show from whence the chords are derived.   (This is not to be played).

Write and play Exercise VII. and Study VII. First put the root on the lower staff, and then the chord on the upper staff.

Exercise VII.

Study VII.

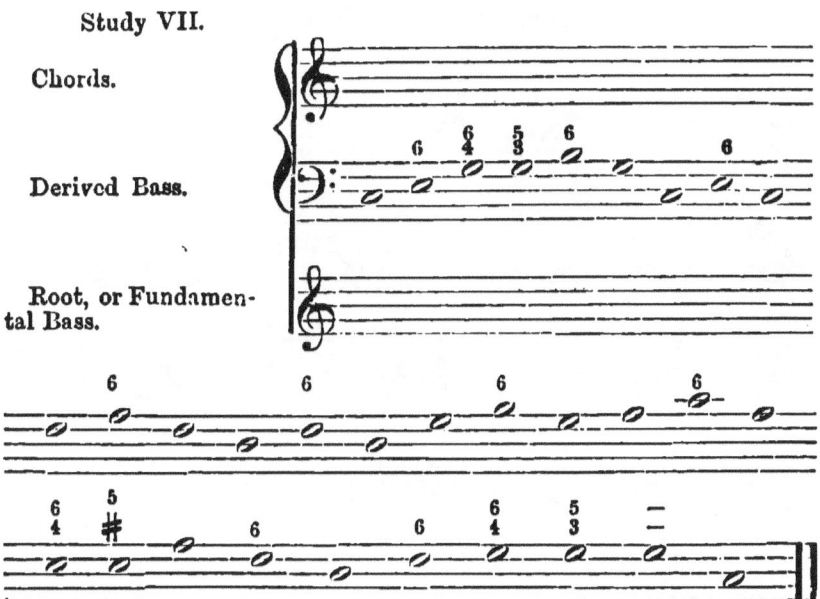

Q. When two or more successive bass notes of the same name occur, and the first of them is figured, is the same chord to be played to them all?

Certainly; the harmony indicated by the preceding figures is to be continued as long as the same bass continues, unless contradicted by a change of figures.

Q. What is meant by two or more following figures over one bass note?

They signify that as many chords are to be played as there are *following* figures; and that the root also is changed each time.

Write and play Exercise VIII. and Study VIII.

Exercise VIII.

Study VIII.

Q. Is it necessary that every note which belongs to a chord should appear in the treble?

No: the note which is in the bass is frequently omitted in the treble, and one of the other intervals is doubled instead of it. This is to be particularly observed when the third is in the bass, (that is, in the chord of the sixth,) especially if it be a major third from the root; for example, the chord of the sixth upon E should be written thus —

Instead of

Q. Is this rule to be observed every time a chord of the sixth occurs?

Not always; when the derived bass is a *minor* third from the root, it may be either doubled or not; but if the derived bass be a major third from the root, it should generally be omitted in the other parts.

Write and play Exercise IX. and Study IX.

Exercise IX.

Study IX

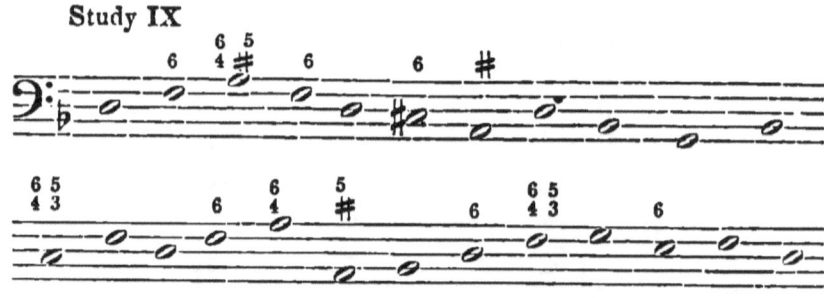

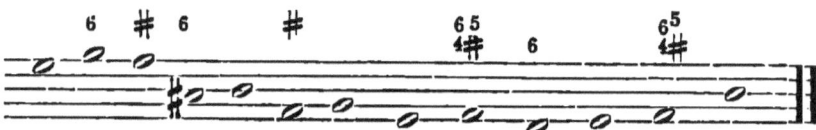

Q. What is the full figuring of the chord of the sixth?

$\frac{8}{6}$; but the figure 6 only is used unless the other intervals require $\frac{8}{6}$ accidentals, as in Exercise X.

Write and play Exercise X.* and Study X.

Exercise X.

*A Sequence, see (Chap. XI.,) which is frequently to be met with, viz., a chord of the 6th followed by a common chord, is introduced in Ex. X. The best mode of accompanying it is to put the octave of the root for the melody, when the third is in the bass, and the third in the melody when the root is in the bass; thus : —

Exercise I. Dominant Sevenths and their resolutions, Major and Minor.

Study X.

Q. What is meant by Contrary Motion ?

It signifies that the chords ascend when the bass descends, or *vice versa.*

Q. What is meant by Similar Motion ?

Similar motion implies that both chords and bass move in the same direction.

Q. What is meant by Oblique Motion ?

It signifies that the chords move while the bass remains stationary, or *vice versa.*

CHAPTER IV.

THE DISCORD OF THE SEVENTH.

Q. What is a Discord?

A discord is a sound which does not form part of the common chord, such as 9, 7, or 4; but the same term is also used to express a combination of sounds in which a discordant note is introduced.

Q. What is meant by the Preparation of a Discord?

A discord is prepared when the discordant note has appeared in the preceding chord; an *added* discord, of course, implies that the discordant note has not appeared in the preceding chord.

Q. What is meant by the Resolution of a Discord?

Every discordant note has a regular progression assigned to it, which is termed its resolution; for example, a ninth must descend to the eighth, a fourth must descend to the third, &c.

Q. How is the Discord of the Seventh produced?

The discord of the seventh consists of the *same notes* as the common chord, (viz., the bass, its third, fifth, and *seventh ;**) consequently it is composed of *four sounds*, and may be taken in four positions.

Q. As the full figuring of the discord of the seventh is $\begin{smallmatrix} 8 \\ 7 \\ 5 \\ 3 \end{smallmatrix}$ is it necessary to use all these figures whenever this chord is intended to be indicated?

No; the 7 alone is sufficient, and the others are only

---

* Observe the seventh is a whole tone below the octave.

4

used when required for the same reasons as the figures of the common chord. (See page 25.)

Q. What is meant by a Dominant Seventh?

It signifies the chord of the fifth of the scale, (which, it has been before remarked, is always a Major Chord,) with the seventh added.

Q. Why is it called the DOMINANT Seventh?

Because it governs or decides the tonic harmony, from its combining those sounds which do not form part of any other scale. Thus G, B, D, and F cannot all be combined in any other scale than that of C major, or C minor. The major chord of G with the seventh, therefore, is termed the dominant seventh of C.

Q. It appears, then, that the dominant seventh governs equally the tonic major and tonic minor.

It does; but it must be observed that, in the minor mode, the third of the dominant is always *raised* by an *accidental*, to form the leading-note of the scale.

Give an example in the key of C minor and other keys.

Q. Should the discordant note, viz., the seventh, ascend or descend?

It must descend either a semitone or a tone. This is called the resolution of the seventh. For example, in the chord of G with the seventh, F must be resolved (that is, descend,) either to E or E♭. See the *white* notes in the following example.

Q. Is there any rule for the progression of either of the other sounds?

Yes; the major third of the dominant (being the leading-note) must ascend a semitone.

Q. What harmony most naturally follows the dominant seventh?

The chord of the tonic, either major or minor; thus G with the dominant seventh will be followed by the chord of C; A with the dominant seventh will be followed by the chord of D, &c., &c.

Write and play dominant sevenths to every note of Exercise I., and let each be properly resolved into the chord of the tonic major, and then minor. Put the requisite figures to the bass notes, and avoid writing them all in the same position. For example : —

[A clear understanding of this exercise being absolutely necessary, the following recapitulation may not be superfluous. First write down the bass note which is to have the dominant seventh—See Exercise I.—and then the bass note which is to follow (viz., the tonic, of which the preceding is dominant.) Write the chord of the dominant seventh in either of the four positions. Resolve the seventh (that is, make it descend,) into the major (or minor) third of the tonic. Resolve the major third of the dominant (that is, make it ascend) into the octave of the tonic. The fifth of the dominant may ascend or descend—(See the black notes, which may be either inserted or omitted;) and the octave of the dominant is to remain, to form the fifth of the tonic.]

Q. As it appears that the root either ascends a fourth or descends a fifth after the dominant seventh, is it the same with those discords of the seventh which have minor thirds?

Yes; the natural progression of all radical or fundamental bass notes, which have been accompanied with sevenths, is to ascend a fourth or descend a fifth.

Write and play Exercise XI. and Study XI.

Exercise XI.

Study XI.

Q. As discords of the seventh are not always prepared, is there any rule to be observed respecting them when taken unprepared ?

Yes; it is *generally* better to descend upon the discordant note than to ascend to it.

Q. When is a discord said to be prepared ?

When the dissonant note has been employed (in the same part) in the preceding chord.

Q. If the octave of the root were omitted in the chord of the dominant seventh, would it occasion the omission of any note in the following chord ?

Yes; the fifth must be omitted in the resolution, otherwise the seventh will ascend, or the third will descend, which is contrary to rule.

Q. Is there any other case in which the fifth is to be omitted ?

Generally when the bass moves one degree upwards or downwards it is necessary to omit the fifth, in order to avoid consecutive fifths. (See second and third chords in Exercise XIII.)

4*

Write and play Exercise XII. and Study XII.

Exercise XII.

Dominant Sevenths with interrupted resolutions, the Bass ascending a tone.

Study XII.

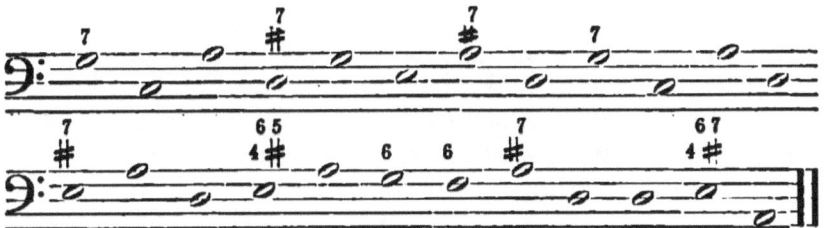

Q. May the seventh be doubled?

No discordant notes should be doubled; for as they have a regular progression assigned to them, they would, if doubled, make consecutive octaves, thus:—

The Fs being sevenths, must descend to Es, thereby producing consecutive octaves.

Q. What is meant by the term, "Interrupted Resolution of the Discord of the Seventh?"

It has been shown in the foregoing examples that the natural progression of the bass notes, which are accompanied with sevenths, is to ascend a fourth or descend a fifth. This is the natural resolution of the harmony; but if the bass ascends only a tone, it is called an *interrupted resolution*.

In this case the dominant seventh, instead of resolving into the harmony of the tonic, resolves into the relative minor.

Q. When a discord of the seventh has an interrupted resolution, should every sound belonging to that discord appear in the accompanying harmony?

No; the octave of the root must be omitted both in the discord of the seventh and following chord, otherwise consecutive octaves with the bass will be made; and the fifth, instead of being at liberty either to ascend or descend, as it may when the resolution is not interrupted, *must* in this case *descend*, in order to prevent consecutive fifths.

Write and play dominant sevenths, in different positions to A, B, C, D, &c. Let the resolutions be interrupted as in the foregoing examples.

Write and play Exercise XIII. and Study XIII.

Exercise XIII.

Dominant Sevenths with interrupted resolutions, the Bass ascending a diatonic semitone.

Study XIII.

Q. Is there any other way of interrupting the resolution of the seventh?

Yes; by making the bass ascend only a diatonic semitone; thus:—

Write and play dominant sevenths in different positions, to A, B, C, D, E, F, G. Interrupt the resolutions by making the bass ascend to a diatonic semitone, as above.

Write and play Exercise XIV. and Study XIV. Point out all those chords of the seventh which have interrupted resolutions.

Exercise XIV.

Study XIV.

CHAPTER V.

THE DERIVATIVES OR INVERSIONS OF THE DISCORD OF THE SEVENTH.

Q. How many chords are derived from the Discord of the Seventh ?

Three ; the $\frac{6}{5}$, the $\frac{6}{3}$, and $\frac{6}{2}$, called the first, second, and third inversions.

Seventh Inversions.

Q. How is the chord of $\frac{6}{5}$ produced ?

By taking the *third* in the bass, instead of the root; for example : —

The root of both these chords is G with the seventh.

Q. How is the chord $\frac{6}{2}$ produced ?

By taking the fifth in the bass, instead of the root; for example : —

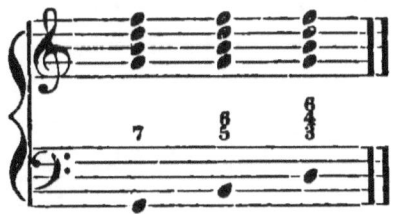

The root of each of these chords is G with the seventh·

Q. How is the chord $\frac{6}{4}$ produced?

By taking the seventh in the bass, instead of the root; for example : —

The root of each of these chords is G with the seventh.

Write and play the chord of the dominant seventh and its derivatives to each note of Exercise I and Study I.

Q. What is the full figuring of the chord $\frac{6}{5}$?

$\frac{6}{5}$, but $\frac{6}{5}$ only are generally used.

Q. When a bass note bears the figures $\frac{6}{5}$, where is the root to be found?

A bass note which bears the figures $\frac{6}{5}$ is to be considered as the third of the root, consequently the root is a third below with a seventh.

Q. In speaking of the chord of the sixth, it was remarked that when the third is used for the bass, it should not appear in the other parts; is this rule to be observed in the $\frac{6}{5}$?

Yes; when the bass note is a *major* third from the root; but when it is a *minor* third from the root, it may or may not be doubled, as the performer chooses.

Q. Is there any exception to this rule?

Yes; when the third is in the bass in two following

chords, it must, to avoid consecutive fifths, appear in the
Treble of only one of them, unless the bass notes be accom-
panied by harmony in two parts only, as in the sequence of
Sixths in page 95.

Write and play Exercises and Studies XV.* and XVI.

Exercise XV.

Study XV.

Exercise XVI.

Study XVI.

What is the full figuring of the chord of the $\begin{smallmatrix}6\\4\\3\end{smallmatrix}$?

$\begin{smallmatrix}8\\6\\4\\3\end{smallmatrix}$, but it is generally abbreviated $\begin{smallmatrix}6\\4\\3\end{smallmatrix}$, or $\begin{smallmatrix}4\\3\end{smallmatrix}$.

Q. Is the figuring of this chord ever abbreviated in any other manner?

Yes; if the sixth be raised a semitone by an accidental sharp or natural, a single ♯6 6̸ or ♮6 is considered to express the whole figures ♯$\begin{smallmatrix}6\\4\\3\end{smallmatrix}$ or ♮$\begin{smallmatrix}6\\4\\3\end{smallmatrix}$.

Write and play Exercises and Studies XVII. and XVIII.

Exercise XVII.

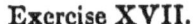

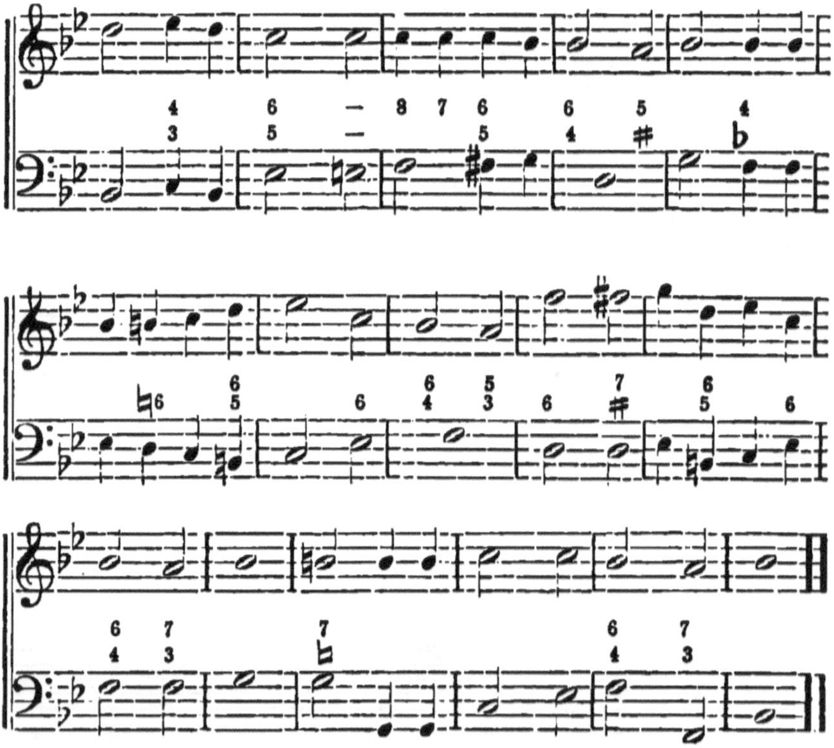

Study XVII.

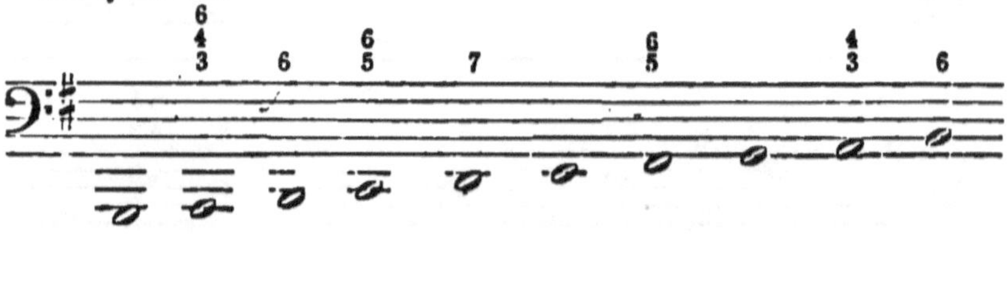

Exercise XVIII.

Study XVIII.

Q. Should every sound belonging to the harmony appear in the chord of the $\frac{6}{4}$?

No; the octave of the root should be omitted; for example:—

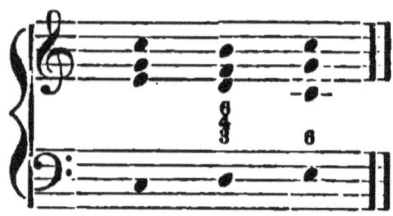

G with the seventh is the root of D; but no G is found in the chord.*

Q. In the foregoing example F, the seventh of the root (instead of descending according to the general rule) ascends to G. Is this correct?

When the bass ascends to the note into which the seventh of the root should resolve, the seventh is, by license, allowed to ascend; consequently as the bass in the preceding example ascends to E, the F may ascend to G.

Write again Exercises and Studies XVII. and XVIII., with particular attention to these rules.

---

* This rule is not invariable; for when the octave of the Root has appeared in the preceding chord, it is sometimes retained in the next.

Q. As the leading-note of any scale cannot be a root on account of its having an imperfect fifth—(See p. 17)—what ought to be considered the root of the second of the scale when it is marked with a 6? In the Key of C, for example, if D (which is the second) be marked with a 6, is the leading-note, B, the root?

No; for when a bass note, supposed to be a root, bearing a common chord, is found to have an imperfect fifth, the real root is a major third below it, bearing a seventh:— Thus the root of D with a 6 according to the general rule, should be B with a common chord; but as B has an imperfect fifth, the root is G with the seventh. Consequently a 6 upon the *second* of the scale must be considered a $\frac{6}{3}$, and the octave of the root (viz., G,) is omitted according to rule.

Q. How is a 6 on the second of the scale of a Major Key to be distinguished from the substituted sixth of the chord of the subdominant of the relative minor, being the same sounds? (See Chap. IX.)

This will be shown by the following chord. If D with a 6 be followed by a chord of C, it is evident that the root of the D is G with the 7th: but if it be followed by E with $\frac{5}{\sharp}$ or with $\frac{6}{4}, \sharp$ it is the substituted Sixth upon the Subdominant, in A Minor.

Write and play Exercises and Studies XIX. and XX.

Exercise XIX.

Study XIX.

Exercise XX.

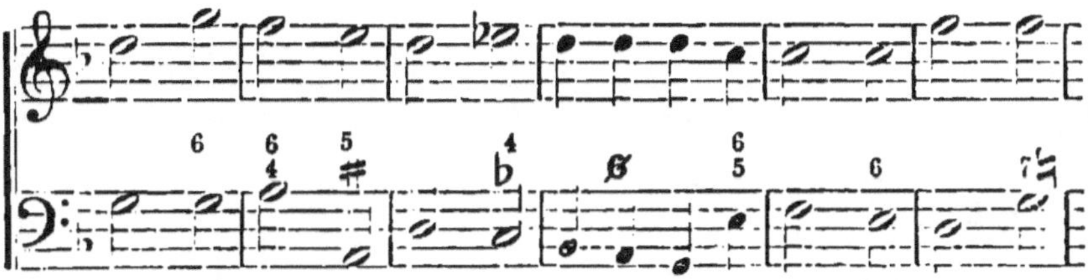

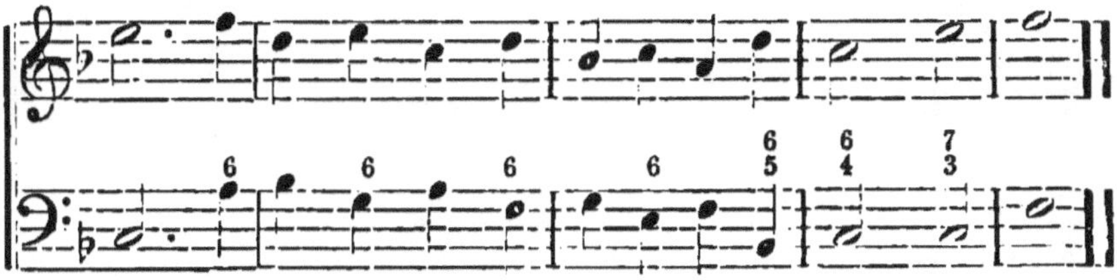

Study XX.

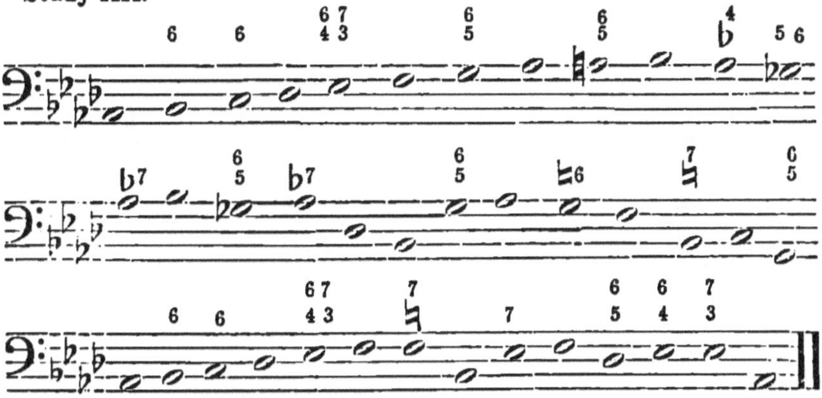

Q. How is the full figuring of the chord $\frac{6}{4}$ abbreviated?

By the figures $\frac{4}{2}$ or with a single 2, and when the fourth is raised a semitone by an accidental sharp or natural, a single #4, or ♮4, suffices to express the whole figures #$\frac{6}{4}$ or ♮$\frac{6}{4}$.

Write and play Exercises and Studies XXI. and XXII.

Exercise XXI.

Study XXI.

Exercise XXII.

Study XXII.

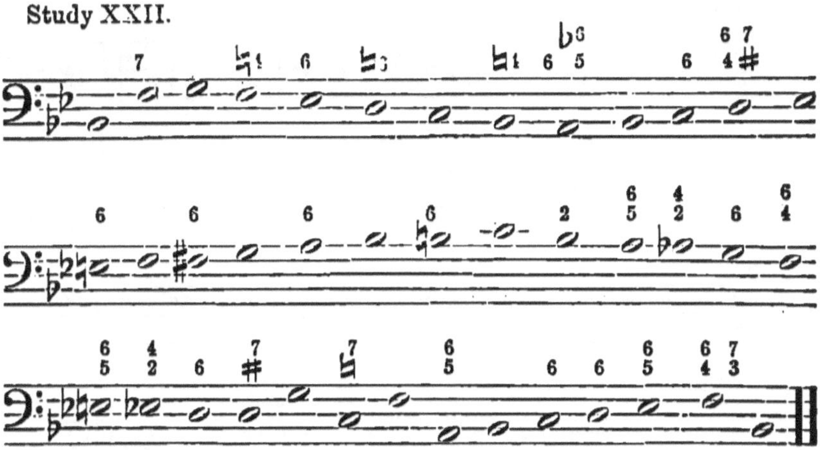

Q. What is meant by passing through the seventh ?

When the harmony of the dominant is followed by the chord of the tonic, the seventh is frequently passed through as in the following example, in which it appears merely as a passing note.

Q. Are two Fifths ever allowed to succeed one another ?

An imperfect may follow a perfect fifth in descending; for example : —

Write and play Exercise and Study **XXIII.**

Exercise XXIII.

Study **XXIII.**

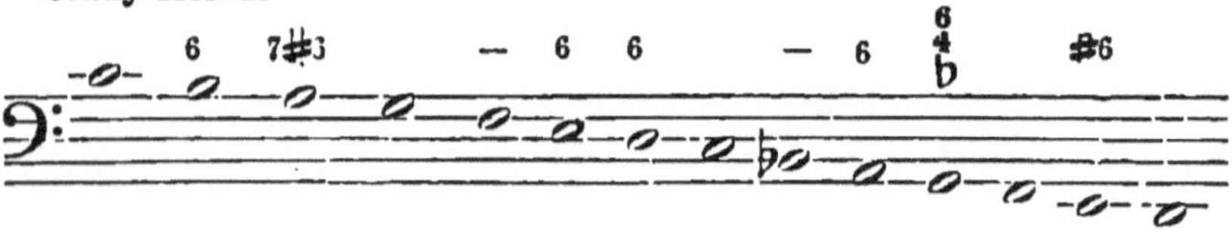

Q. Does a single 5, ♭5, or ♮5 over a bass note always imply the common chord?

Not if the fifth so implied be *imperfect;* for example, if there are no flats or sharps at the signature, all the following marks imply *imperfect* fifths: —

consequently they cannot be considered as roots.

Q. Where then is the root to be found?

The root is to be found as already described in relation to the root of the leading note; therefore the above marks are to be considered as abbreviations of the figures $\frac{6}{5}$.

Write and play Exercise and Study XXIV.

Exercise **XXIV.**

Study XXIV.

Q. Must the Leading-note (viz., the major third of the dominant,) always ascend ?

Its natural progression is to ascend; but when the seventh is taken in two following chords, the leading-note of the first is allowed to descend a chromatic semitone, which forms the seventh of the next; for example :—

Q. If the leading-note is in the bass, as in the chord of the ⁶₅, is it in that case allowed to descend ?

Yes; according to the same rule; for example:—

Q. In what case may the seventh be doubled?

It is sometimes doubled in the chord of the $\frac{6}{4}$$_3$ in preference to taking the octave of the root, in this case the lower one is made to ascend, in order to avoid the octaves; for example: —

Write and play Exercise and Study XXV.

Exercise XXV.

Study XXV.

CHAPTER VI.

DISCORDS BY SUSPENSION.

A Discord by Suspension occurs when some note or notes of one chord are retained in the next chord, instead of taking at once the harmony belonging to the root of the next chord; by which means the harmony of that root is for a time suspended. Thus the eighth is suspended by the ninth, which is produced by retaining the fifth of the dominant in the following (tonic) chord (Example 1.) The third is suspended by the fourth, which is produced by retaining the eighth of the tonic on the following (dominant) chord (Example 2.)

The chords, except the suspended notes, are to be considered as common chords, the ninth being used instead of the eighth; the chord is in all other respects to be treated as if it were not used. The same is to be observed when the fourth is used instead of the third.

Q. May the ninth and eighth appear in a chord at the same time?

No; if there be any sound in the preceding chord which ought to be resolved by the eighth, the ninth cannot properly be played with it; for instance, in the example marked "prepared by the fifth," the B in the chord of G being the major third, should ascend to C, consequently the ninth ought not to be used.

Q. May the discords of the ninth and the fourth be used without preparation?

Generally speaking, they should be prepared; although instances may be met with when they are not so.

Q. Must they be resolved?

Yes; both ninth and fourth must be resolved, by descending either a semitone or a tone.

Q. Is it necessary that the resolution of a discord should take place in the next chord?

No; the resolution is frequently suspended for a time; for example:—

but in every discord by suspension the discordant note should ultimately resolve into the note which it suspended.

Write and play Exercises and Studies **XXVI.** and **XXVII.**

Exercise XXVI.

Study XXVI.

Exercise XXVII.

Study XXVII.

Q. Is there any rule for the preparation of the discords of the fourth and the ninth?

The fourth may be prepared by any interval except the second; but the ninth must not be prepared by the eighth on account of its making *hidden* octaves, as may be seen in the following example: —

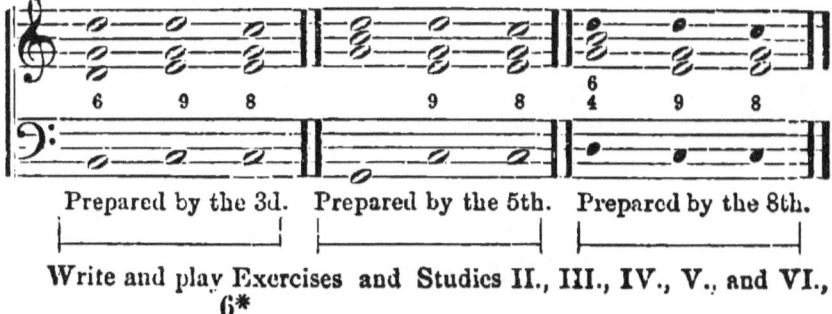

Prepared by the 3d.   Prepared by the 5th.   Prepared by the 8th.

Write and play Exercises and Studies II., III., IV., V., and VI.,

6*

and insert fourths and ninths wherever they can be admitted, taking care to prepare and resolve them properly.

Q. Are the ninth and fourth ever used at the same time instead of the eighth and third?

Yes; for example:—

Write and play Exercise and Study **XXVIII.**

Exercise **XXVIII.**

Study XXVIII.

Write and play Exercises XV. and XVI. and insert the Discord of the $\frac{9}{4}$, wherever it can be admitted.

Are the discords of the ninth and fourth ever used with the discord of the seventh.

Yes; the $\frac{7}{4}$ occurs frequently, but the $\frac{9}{7}$ is not often used when the root is taken in the bass, though it is frequently taken upon one of the derivatives or inversions.

Q. Is the ninth always a tone above the octave?

No; it is sometimes a semitone, in which case it is called a flat ninth. It should be remarked, that the $\frac{9}{7}$ resolves into the harmony of the tonic major, and the $\flat\frac{9}{7}$ resolves (generally, but not always.) into the harmony of the tonic minor—for example:

Q. What is the natural progression of the root after the $\frac{9}{7}$?

It is the same as after a dominant seventh, viz., it either ascends a fourth, or descends a fifth; for $\frac{9}{7}$ is only a suspension of $\frac{8}{7}$, consequently it makes no difference in the progression of the root.

Write and play Exercises and Studies XXIX. and XXX.

Exercise **XXIX.**

Study **XXIX.**

Exercise XXX.

Study XXX.

Q. What is the chord of the $\frac{5}{2}$?

It is an inversion of $\frac{5}{4}$; for the $\frac{5}{4}$ suspends the common chord, by taking the *fourth* instead of the *third* in the *treble*, and $\frac{5}{2}$ suspends the chord of the sixth (which, it must be remembered, is produced by taking the third in the bass,) by taking the *fourth* instead of the *third* in the *Bass*; for example:—

Q. Is a bass note when marked $\frac{5}{2}$ a root?

No; it is the fourth of another note; and it must be remembered that the fourth being used *instead* of the third in the bass, is thereby excluded from the harmony.

Write and play Exercises and Studies **XXXI.** and **XXXII.**

Exercise **XXXI.**

Study XXXI.

Exercise XXXII.

Study XXXII.

[musical notation with figured bass]

CHAPTER VII.

CHORD OF THE DIMINISHED SEVENTH.

Q. How is the chord of the Diminished Seventh produced ?

It may be produced by taking any chord of the dominant seventh, and raising the bass a chromatic semitone ; for example : —

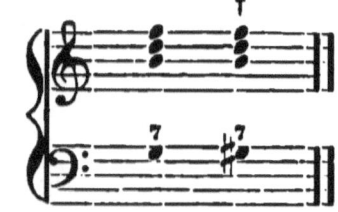

Q. How does it happen that the same sounds are used to accompany G with the Seventh, and G♯ with the Seventh ?

It is a rule that no accidentals should be used, unless they are expressed by the figures ; consequently the third, fifth and seventh to G, or G♯, will be B, D, and F, there being no flats or sharps at the signature. If the harmony of the *dominant* seventh were required to the G♯, it would be necessary to mark it thus : —

Q. As the chord of the diminished seventh has an imperfect fifth —(See the examplet)—is the root to be found in the manner described in page 48 ?

Yes; except that the supposed root in that case appears to bear a common chord, but having an imperfect fifth, the real root is a major third lower with the seventh; whereas in the present instance the supposed root bears a seventh, therefore the real root is a major third lower, with the $\frac{9}{7}$.

Repeat both rules.

When that which is supposed to be the root, bearing a common chord, is found to have an imperfect fifth, the real root is a major third below, and bears a seventh.

When that which is supposed to be the root, bearing a seventh, is found to have an imperfect fifth, the real root is a major third below, and bears a $\frac{9}{7}$.

Write and play Exercises and Studies XXXIII., XXXIV., and XXXV.*

Exercise XXXIII.

* The melody of GOD SAVE THE KING may be played to this Exercise.

Study XXXIII.

Exercise XXXIV.

Study XXXIV.

Exercise XXXV.

Study XXXV.

Q. How many chords are derived from the diminished seventh?

Three; viz., the $\#^6_5, \#^6_{4_3}$, and $^6_{\#2}$; for example: —

The figures to all these chords denote them to be derived from G♯ with the seventh; but for the reason before given, the real root is E, with the $\frac{9}{7}$.

Q. Are the same rules to be observed with these chords as with the derivatives of the dominant seventh?

Yes; therefore when the major third of the *real root* is in the bass, it must not appear in any other part, neither must the discordant notes (viz., the seventh or ninth of the real root) be doubled.

Write and play Exercises and Studies **XXXVI.** and **XXXVII.**

Exercise **XXXVI.**

Study XXXVI.

Exercise XXXVII.

7*

Study XXXVII.

CHAPTER VIII.

CHORD OF THE EXTREME SHARP SIXTH.

Q. How is the chord of the Extreme Sharp Sixth produced?

It may be produced by taking the chord of the ♮6 or ♯6 — viz., $\frac{6}{4}$ — and lowering the bass a chromatic semitone; for example:—

The bass in this chord must be considered as lowered by license, and the chords must be treated in all respects, and the root found, as if the bass were not lowered. In the foregoing example, the root of E is clearly A with $\overset{7}{\sharp}$; the root of the E♭ must also be considered the same (viz., A,) the E being lowered by license.

Q. What is the natural resolution of this chord?

Its resolution is the same as the $\sharp^6$, viz., the *root* ascends a fourth; therefore the E♭ in the foregoing example will resolve into the chord of D major, and the D♮ will resolve into the chord of C major.

Q. Is there any rule for the progression of a bass note which bears the chord of the extreme sharp sixth?

Yes; it must descend a diatonic semitone, and its most usual resolution is into a *major* chord; for example: —

Q. How is the performer to decide whether the chord of the sharp sixth, or the chord of the extreme sharp sixth is intended?

The signature will determine it, as will be seen from the following example: —

The plain 6 in the latter case implies the chord of the extreme sharp sixth, the C being sharp by the signature.

Write and play Exercises and Studies XXXVIII. and XXXIX.

Exercise XXXVIII.

Study XXXVIII.

Exercise XXXIX.

Study XXXIX.

Q. May the ninth of the root be taken with the chord of the extreme sharp sixth? (See the white notes.)

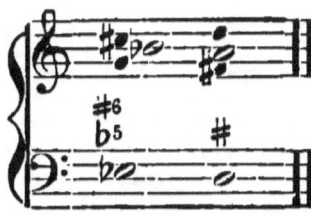

No; because B♮ being the ninth of the root, descends to

A; making perfect fifths with the bass, which also must descend.

Q. Is there any case in which the ninth of the root can be taken with the chord of the extreme sharp sixth?

It is sometimes done when an intermediate chord is inserted between the extreme sharp sixth and its resolution; thus: —

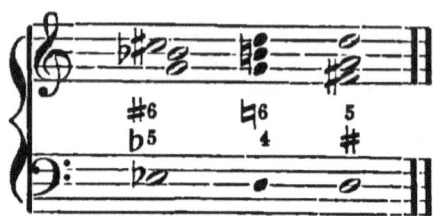

The ♮⁶₄, which is here taken upon the chord of D, must be considered as a suspension of the chord of D, for the root after the E♭ must be D.*

Write and play Exercises and Studies XL. and XLI.

Exercise XL.

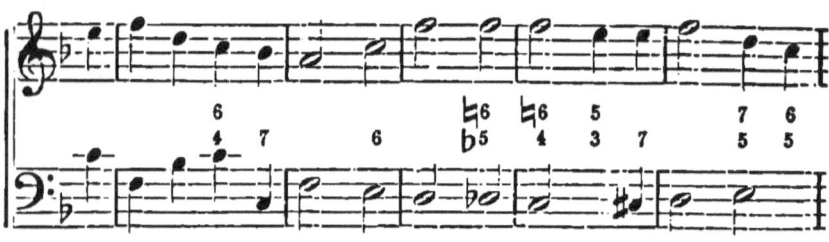

---

* This is one of many exceptions which might be given to the general rules, but the Author has avoided them as much as possible in the present little volume; conceiving that the ground-work of Harmony should be first thoroughly understood, before the varieties of which it is susceptible are attempted to be acquired.

Study XL.

Exercise XLI.

Study XLI.

CHAPTER IX.

CADENCES.

Q. What is the rule for making a Cadence or Close?

A Cadence, in its most simple form, consists of the harmonies of the sub-dominant, dominant, (viz., the attendant harmonies) and tonic; for example: —

But as the progression from the chord of the subdominant to the dominant is harsh, the tonic harmony is frequently inserted upon the dominant bass, previous to its own chord; thus: —

and the seventh is generally added to the harmony of the dominant, as in the foregoing example.

Make cadences, with the chords in different positions, in G, D, E♭, F♯, &c. Make some with and some without inserting the $\frac{6}{4}$ upon the dominant.

Q. Is there any other way of varying the cadence and avoiding the harshness in the progression from the subdominant to the dominant?

Yes; by means of what is called the substituted sixth.

Q. What is meant by the Substituted Sixth?

The chord of the substituted sixth is produced by making the subdominant bear the chord of the sixth, instead of its common chord.

8

Make cadences with the substituted sixth on the subdominant, in A, E, B♭, D♭, &c. Let the dominant in some bear the chords of the $\frac{6}{4}$, $\frac{5}{3}$, in others the $\frac{6}{4}$, $\frac{7}{3}$, the $\frac{5}{4}$ $\frac{5}{3}$, or the $\frac{6}{4}$, $\frac{5}{4}$, $\frac{7}{3}$.

The sixth is sometimes *added* to the chord of the subdominant, instead of being *substituted* for the fifth; thus :—

Q. What is the difference between the chord of the substituted sixth and the first inversion of the MINOR common chord, and how should the root be marked ?

A bass note marked 6, when followed by a note one tone above it, should be considered part of a cadence, as it must ultimately bear its major chord with or without the seventh; for instance, if F, marked 6, is followed by G with its major chord, or with $\frac{6}{4}$ $\frac{5}{3}$, or with $\frac{5}{4}$ $\frac{5}{3}$, the F is then the root and should be marked 6. This explanation applies also to the added sixth $\frac{5}{6}$, and although F with $\frac{5}{6}$ be set down as the root, the chord must be treated as the first inversion of D, with the seventh; consequently the C should, if possible, be prepared and resolved by descending.

Q. Is there any other method of varying the cadence ?

Yes; the subdominant is sometimes raised a chromatic semitone, and the chord of the diminished seventh taken upon it; see following example :—

But this, and others which are sometimes used, may be considered as variations upon the common or authentic cadence, the basis of which is the SUBDOMINANT, DOMINANT, and TONIC.

The pupil will make cadences with the $\frac{6}{5}$ on the subdominant, also with the diminished 7th on the RAISED subdominant, as above described in B, A♭, E♭, &c.

Q. What is meant by an Authentic Cadence?

When the tonic harmony is preceded by the harmony of the dominant, it is termed an authentic cadence; the foregoing are all authentic cadences.

Q. What is meant by a Plagal Cadence?

A plagal cadence signifies that the tonic harmony is preceded by the harmony of the subdominant.

Give examples in various keys.

Q. How is a cadence to be made in a minor key?

In the same manner as in a major key, viz., by the harmonies of the subdominant, dominant, and tonic; observing that the chords of the subdominant and tonic are minor, and that the chord of the dominant must be made major by an accidental; for example:—

The seventh may or may not be added to the chord of the dominant, as above.

Make a cadence in some other minor key.

Q. Is the substituted sixth ever used in making a cadence in a minor key?

Yes; for example :—

Q. What is meant by a Half Cadence ?

A half cadence is made by ending a passage upon the harmony of the dominant, preceded by the harmony of the tonic. It is used for phrases which are not final; as it does not end on the tonic, it has an unfinished effect; example :—

Or,

Make a half cadence in some other key.

Q. How is an interrupted cadence made ?

It may be done in the same way that the resolution of

the dominant seventh is interrupted, viz., by making the bass ascend a semitone or tone, instead of going to the tonic; for example : —

There are many ways of varying, as well as interrupting the cadence, which will be seen in the Exercises.

The interrupted cadence is not a *close*, but rather a temporary evasion of the final close, which eventually follows.

CHAPTER X.

CHORD OF THE SEVENTH, FOURTH, AND SECOND, &C.

Q. How is the chord $\frac{7}{4}$ produced ?

By taking the chord of the dominant seventh upon the tonic bass. For example, the chord of G with the seventh upon C in the bass, or D with the seventh upon G in the bass, as in the following example : —

Q. What is the resolution of the chord $\frac{7}{4}$?

It resolves into the harmony of the tonic. See the above examples.

8*

Write and play the chord $\frac{7}{4}_2$ and its resolution upon D, E, F, G, &c., taking care to put the proper accidentals to notes and figures belonging to the various keys.

Write and play Exercises and Studies XLII. and XLIII.

Exercise XLII.

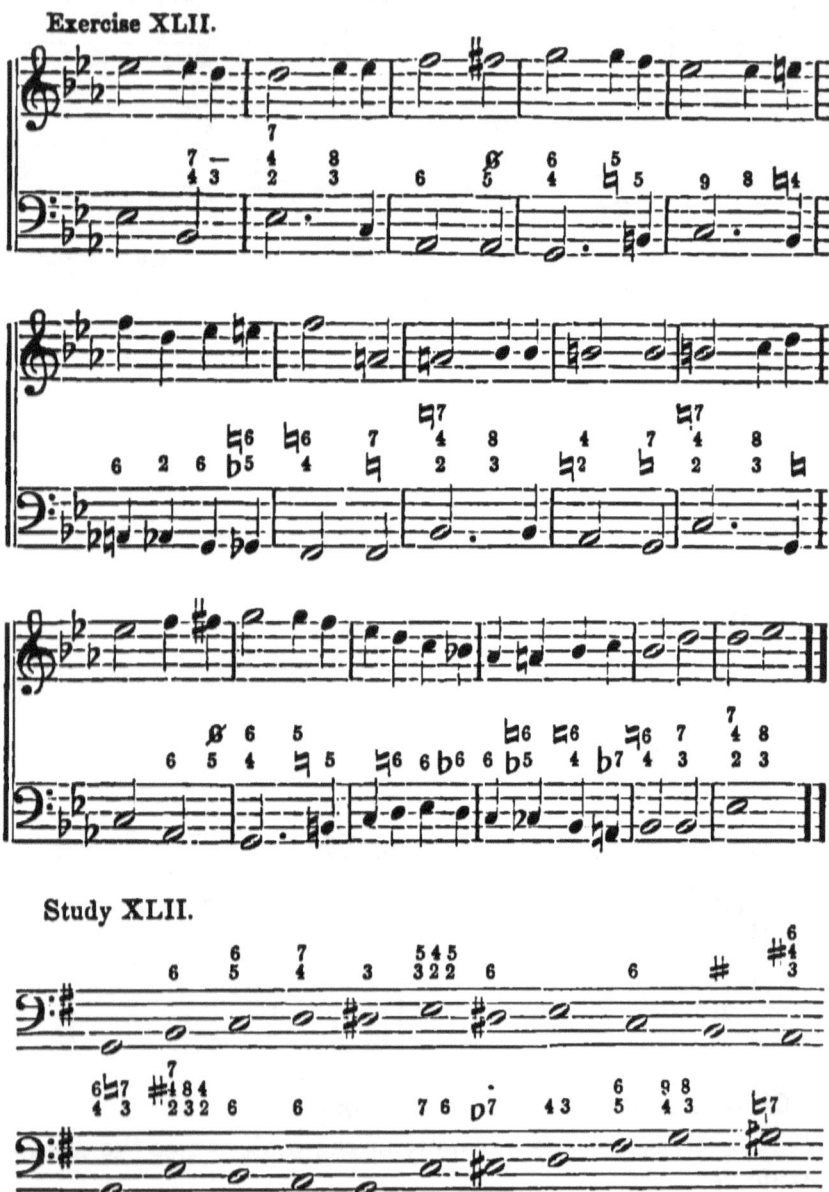

Study XLII.

Q. How is the chord of $\begin{smallmatrix}7\\6\\4\\2\end{smallmatrix}$ produced ?

In the same manner as the preceding chord, and differs from it only by taking the *flat ninth* instead of the *octave* of the root; for example, G with b♭$\begin{smallmatrix}9\\7\end{smallmatrix}$ upon C in the bass, or D with the b♭$\begin{smallmatrix}9\\7\end{smallmatrix}$ upon G in the bass.

Q. What is the resolution of the chord $\begin{smallmatrix}7\\6\\4\\2\end{smallmatrix}$?

It resolves into the harmony of the tonic. See the above examples.

Write and play the chord of $\begin{smallmatrix}7\\6\\4\\2\end{smallmatrix}$ and ·its resolution to D, A, F, B, &c., taking care to put the requisite accidentals to the notes and figures.

Write and play Exercise and Study XLIV.

Exercise XLIV.

Study XLIV.

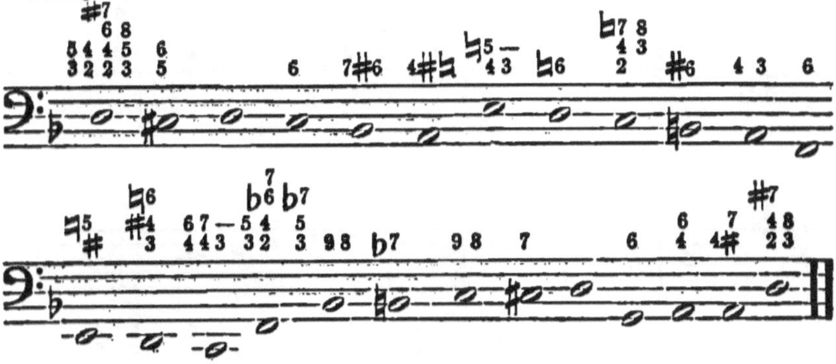

Q. What is meant by a Pedal Bass ?

When one bass note is held or repeated to several different chords, it is called a pedal base ; for example :—

All the discords, it is to be observed, must be resolved in the same manner as if their respective roots were played instead of the pedal bass.

Write and play Exercise and Study XLV.

Exercise XLV.

Study XLV.

Q. What is meant by a Ground Bass?

It signifies a series of bass notes repeated several times, with a different accompaniment each time.

See Exercise and Study XLVI.

CHAPTER XI.

SEQUENCES.

Q. What is a Sequence?

A sequence is a succession or series of chords of the same species, consisting in some cases of single chords and in others of two chords, usually accompanied with two-part harmony, on a uniform progression in the bass.

Give an example of a sequence of sixths.

By suspending the upper notes a sequence of sevenths and sixths may be produced; thus: —

This example *may* be considered as a variation of the former, made by suspending the upper notes; but it is more regular in a sequence of sevenths and sixths to con-sider the sixths as chords of the $\frac{6}{3}$, consequently the roots of the foregoing example are: —

This will also serve as a specimen of a sequence of sevenths.

It has been remarked in the preceding pages that a bass note, which has an imperfect fifth, cannot be a root; this rule, however, is subject to some exceptions, for in sequences, especially when confined to one scale, both the *imperfect common chord* (which consists of the note itself, minor third, and *imperfect* fifth) and its inversions are admitted and treated as ordinary major and minor chords. See foregoing example.

In sequences, for the sake of symmetrical movement of the parts, strict adherence to the rules for resolving discords is dispensed with.

In addition to the two discords of the seventh already described, there are two others to be mentioned, viz., one with a *major* seventh and the other with an *imperfect* fifth. The following sequence employs the discord of the seventh upon every note of the diatonic scale.

It will be seen that the dominant (G) is the only note which has a major third, perfect fifth, and minor seventh.

The second (D,) third (E,) and sixth (A) have each a minor third, perfect fifth, and minor seventh.

The tonic (C) and subdominant (F) have each a major

third, perfect fifth, and *major* seventh, and the leading-note
(B) has a minor third, *imperfect* fifth, and minor seventh.
Such combinations are subject to the same rules as the
dominant seventh, and seldom used except in sequences.

Q. Is a sequence of sixths ever used in ascending ?

Yes; for example : —

This may be varied into a sequence of fifths and sixths;
thus : —

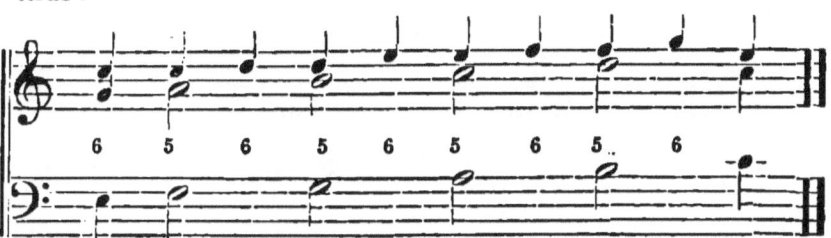

Write and play Exercises and Studies XLVI., XLVII., XLVIII.,
and XLIX.

Exercise XLVI.

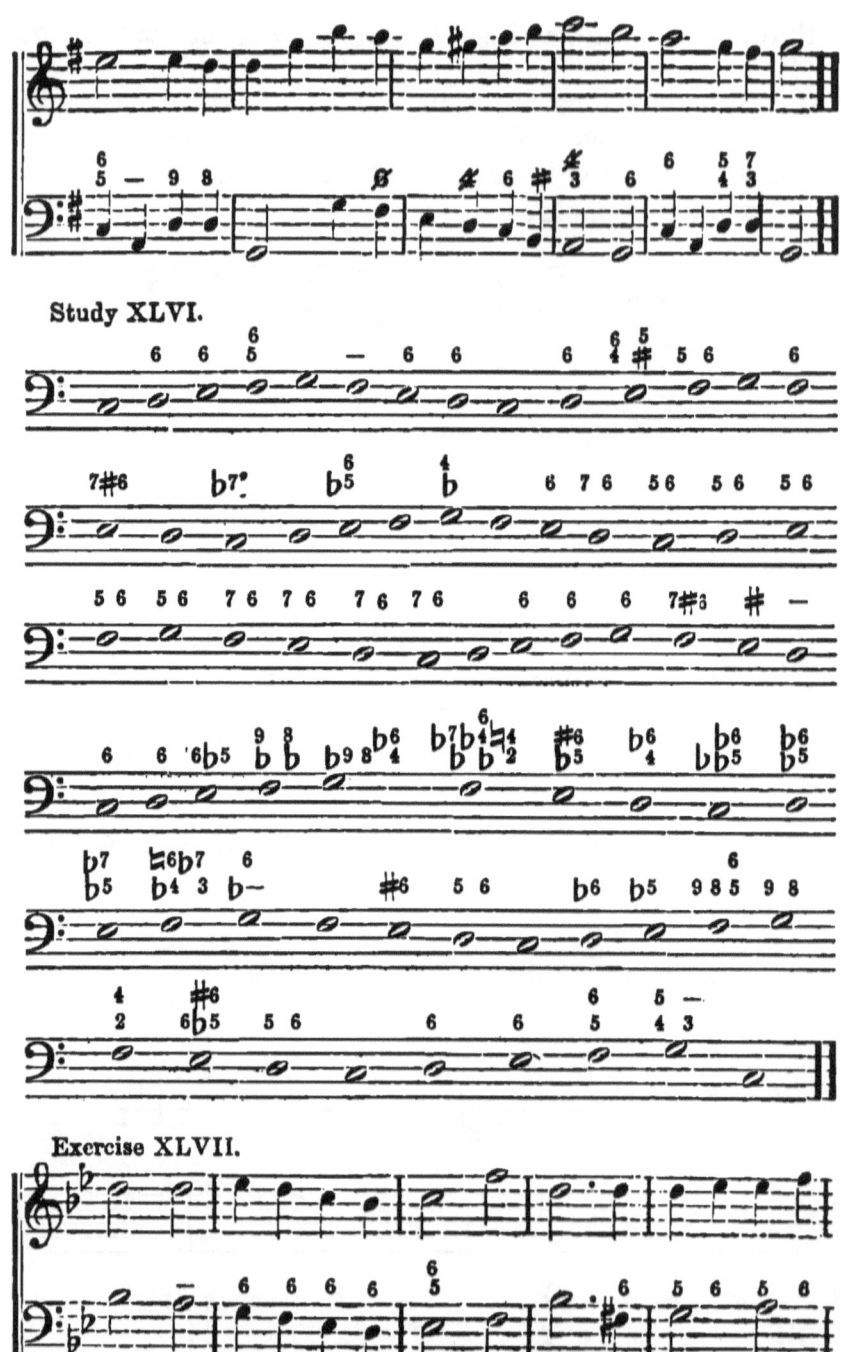

Study XLVI.

Exercise XLVII.

Study XLVII.

Exercise XLVIII.

Study XLVIII.

Exer cise XLIX.

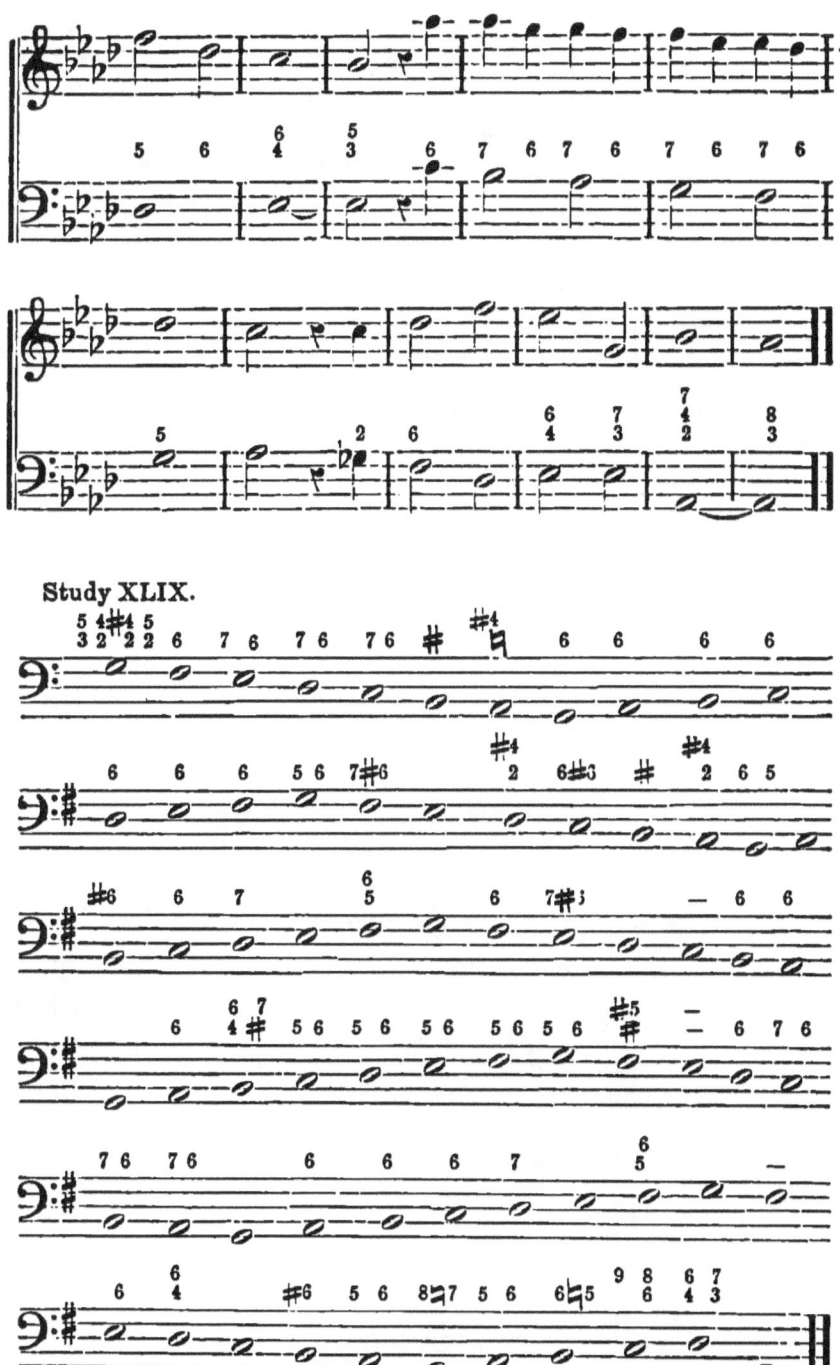

Study XLIX.

Sequences are sometimes figurative, or embellished with extraneous notes which are not integral portions of the harmony, but should preserve the same symmetrical form or figure throughout.　Example: —

&c.

Q. When chords are written to bass notes which are not figured, how is it to be ascertained what chords they are and what are their roots?

Reckon at what intervals the written notes are from the bass, taking no notice of those sounds which are doubled; this will give the full figuring, from which the root may be found in the usual manner.　The essential figures only must be written, for the reasons already given.

Q. What is the proper figuring and root of this chord?

It will be seen that F is the seventh, B the third, D the imperfect fifth; the full figuring then is $\frac{7}{5}$, consequently a $_3$
7 is the only figure necessary to be written.　The root at first may be supposed to be G$\sharp$ with the seventh, but for the reason given in page 59, it is E with the $\frac{9}{7}$.
$\sharp$

Q. What is the proper figuring and root of the following?

E♯ is the ♯6, B the third, D the imperfect fifth; the full figuring is ♯6/5/3; the essential figures ♯6/♯5, the root C♯ with the 9/7/♯.

Q. What is the proper figuring and root of

F is the sixth, B the second, D the fourth; the full figuring is 6/4/2; the essential figures 4/2, the root G with the ♭9/7.

Q. What is the full figuring and root of

F is the sixth, C♭ the flat third, D the fourth; the full figuring is 6/4; the essential figures ♭4; the root B♭ with the ♭9/♭7.

Add the requisite figures, and name the roots of the chords of Exercise L.

CHAPTER XII.

OF MODULATION, &C.

Q. What is meant by Modulation?

Modulation is a change of key produced by the introduction of harmonies which do not belong to the original key.

Q. What is a Transition?

A transition also signifies a change of key.

Q. What then is the difference between a Modulation and a Transition?

A modulation from one key to another is made by using those chords which are common to both, or those which are nearest to them, by which the ear is gradually prepared for the new key; but a transition is made by going suddenly from one key to another, without any preparatory intervening chords; for example, from C to A♭.

Q. What are the most usual modulations?

The most usual are from the tonic to the dominant, subdominant, or relative minor.

Q. How is it to be ascertained when a modulation is made from one key to another?

The most decisive proof is the chord of the dominant seventh (or any of its inversions); this one chord determines the tonic from its combining (as before remarked) all the sounds, which prove that it is not in either of the keys related to that which might be supposed; for example, the dominant seventh upon G proves that the tonic can be no other than C (either major or minor), for the following reasons: —

The F ♮ proves it is not G (the dominant.)

The B♮ proves it is not in F (the subdominant.)

The G♮ proves it is not in A minor (the relative minor.)

Q. Is there any other way of knowing what key is modulated into?

Yes; the chords of the subdominant and dominant combine the sounds before mentioned, and thus determine the tonic.

Q. Is not the chord of the tonic itself a certain indication of a key ?

Not alone: for example, the chord of C is common to the keys of C, G, and F ; therefore unless it is accompanied with some other chords, it is by no means certain that the piece is in the key of C.

Q. In what manner is a modulation to be made from the tonic to the dominant?

By raising the fourth of the scale a chromatic semitone ; therefore a modulation from the key of C to the key of G is made by introducing F♯. The return from the dominant to the tonic must be made by lowering the seventh of the *new scale* a chromatic semitone; consequently the return from G to C must be made by introducing F♮. See following example.

Modulate from various keys to their dominants and back again.

Q. How is a modulation to be made from the tonic to the subdominant ?

Exactly the reverse of the former; that is to say, in order to modulate from the tonic to the subdominant, the seventh must be lowered a chromatic semitone; and to return, the fourth of the subdominant must be raised again ; therefore a modulation from the key of C to the key of F must be made by introducing B♭ ; and the return from F to C by introducing B♮ ; for example : —

Tonic to subdominant and back.

Modulate from various keys to their subdominants and back again.

Q. How is a modulation to be made from the tonic to the relative minor?

By raising the fifth of the scale a chromatic semitone; therefore a modulation from the key of C to the key of A minor is made by introducing G♯; and the return must be made by introducing G♮.

Modulate from various keys to their relative minors and back again.

Q. How are other modulations to be made?

The methods of modulating from one key to another are so various, that it is impossible to give any general rule.

The Author thinks it necessary to remark that the subsequent examples and observations upon modulation are not inserted as models for imitation, but are introduced for no other purpose than to give the student a habit of thinking upon the subject.

A modulation may be made from any major chord to its relative minor, by taking the chord of the ♯6 upon the semitone below; thus:—

By this means, therefore, modulations may be made from the tonic, either to its relative minor or the relative minors of its dominant or subdominant.

A modulation from any major chord to its dominant may be made by taking the chord of the ♯4 (viz., the ♯$^4_2$) upon the same bass note.

From any minor chord a cadence may be easily made, either in its own key, into its relative major, or the dominant of its relative major; thus:—

Any major chord, as a dominant, governs equally the tonic major and the tonic minor; for example, the chord of C governs F major and F minor.

Sometimes an abrupt change is made from the tonic major to the tonic minor, or *vica versa*.

By changing a dominant seventh into a diminished seventh, a modulation may be made into the relative minor, for example:

By an interrupted resolution of the dominant seventh a modulation may be made into the minor sixth of the scale; thus G with the seventh is the dominant of C, but by the interrupted resolution it goes into A♭; for example:—

The chord of the extreme sharp sixth resolves into the major chord of the semitone below; in the key of C, therefore, the ♯6 upon the tonic will resolve into B major; upon the dominant into F♯ major; and upon the subdominant into E major: for example:—

Exercise 50 is inserted to show how a Modulation may be made from C to every note of the diatonic scale, major and minor.

From C to D.

From C to D minor.

From C to E.

From C to E minor.

10

From C to A minor.

From C to B.

From C to B minor.

Study L.

From C, to D♭.　　　From C, to D♭ Minor.

&c.　　　&c.

Study L. is inserted to show in what manner a modulation *may* be made from the key of C to every note of the chromatic scale, major and minor. Each piece should be written and played several times, and the student should add a different termination each time, in the following manner :

To those which are from C to a major key, first make a cadence in the key desired; secondly, make a cadence in the relative minor; thirdly, in the dominant of the key desired; fourthly, in the subdominant of the key desired.

To those which are marked from C to a minor key, first make a cadence in the key desired; secondly, in the relative major; thirdly, in the dominant of the relative major.

The cadences should be varied, and occasionally interrupted; the student should also be required to modulate from C to any other key, in another and less sudden manner than that set down. When this is done with a tolerable degree of facility, exercises may be given in the following manner : —

Modulate from any key (major or minor) to any other key (major or minor), and back again.

Q. What is meant by writing in parts ?

It signifies writing for several voices or instruments. Each part is generally written on a separate staff.

Q. What is Counterpoint?

Counterpoint is the art of arranging the sounds belonging to the harmony, so that each has its proper progression.

Q. What is Simple Counterpoint ?

Simple counterpoint implies that the notes in each part are of equal duration.

Q. What is Figurative Counterpoint ?

Figurative counterpoint implies that the parts consist of notes differing from each other in value.

Q. What are Passing Notes ?

Passing notes are those which move from one harmony to another, without forming a component part of either.

Q. What is meant by Music in Score ?

It signifies a piece composed for several voices or instruments (or both), written on several staves one over another, according to the number of parts, so that the whole which is intended to be performed by the several voices or instruments may be seen at one view.

Q. What is meant by playing from Score?

Playing from score signifies playing music written as above described, and giving as nearly as possible the general effect of the whole composition upon one instrument.

Q. What is meant by Tasto Solo, or T. S.?

It signifies that the passage which is so marked is to be played exactly as it is written; that is to say, no chords are to be added.

Q. How is a passage to be played which is marked Únis, or Unison?

It literally means that all the parts are in unison, and no chords are to be played; the passages so marked are generally performed in octaves.

In the foregoing pages it has been the Author's chief endeavor to unite the utmost brevity with the pupil's instruction. ·Should he be found to have erred in this respect, he will still flatter himself that they who have made themselves acquainted with his work will find no difficulty in understanding other works, which, from their extent, admit of much greater detail.

www.ingramcontent.com/pod-product-compliance
Lightning Source LLC
Chambersburg PA
CBHW022340020726
47500CB00004B/1212